ELIZABETH RING

PERFORMING DOGS

STARS OF STAGE, SCREEN, AND TELEVISION

GOOD DOGS!
THE MILLBROOK PRESS ▪ BROOKFIELD, CONNECTICUT

FOR JENI:
RISING STAR

Cover photo courtesy of Sygma
Photos courtesy of © Douglas Kirk: pp. 3, 10, 23, 27;
Museum of Modern Art Film Stills Archive: pp. 4, 9;
Archive Photos: pp. 7, 12, 14, 25; © Touchstone Televi-
sion: p. 17; Robert Marston Corporate Communications:
p. 18; Bashkim Dibra: p. 19; Zoo Shows: p. 21.

Library of Congress Cataloging-in-Publication Data
Ring, Elizabeth, 1920–
Performing dogs : stars of stage, screen, and television /
by Elizabeth Ring.
p.   cm.—(Good dogs!)
Includes bibliographical references and index.
Summary: Takes the reader behind the scenes for a
look at our most famous canine performers, their trainers,
and the roles that made them famous.
ISBN 1-56294-296-4 (lib. bdg.)
1. Dogs in the performing arts—United States—Juvenile
literature.   2. Dogs—Training—Juvenile literature.
[1. Dogs in the performing arts.   2. Dogs—Training.]
I. Title.   II. Series:
Ring, Elizabeth, 1920–   Good dogs!
PN1590.D63R56   1994
791.8—dc20   93-41964   CIP   AC

Published by The Millbrook Press
2 Old New Milford Road
Brookfield, Connecticut 06804

PERFORMING DOGS

Terry as Toto and Judy Garland as Dorothy
in a publicity photo for *The Wizard of Oz.*

Across the flat Kansas plains, a tornado twists—like a huge black snake dancing on its tail. Dorothy, a girl who lives on a farm, runs down a dusty road. She is clutching her little dog Toto to her, racing to get home before the storm swoops down.

She reaches the farmhouse and plunges inside. ''Auntie Em! Auntie Em!'' Dorothy calls.

But Auntie Em is not there. Everyone on the farm is underground in a shelter. It is too late for Dorothy to join them. The tornado roars by like a speeding freight train. The storm shakes the house, smashes windows and doors.

Toto is almost blown away. Then Dorothy is hit on the head and knocked unconscious. She dreams that the house is being swirled into the sky and that she and Toto are being carried off somewhere. Soon she finds herself in the ''land of Oz.''

In the dream, Toto trots down a yellow brick road alongside Dorothy, the Scarecrow, the Tin Man, and the Cowardly Lion. In their adventures in Oz, Toto escapes the clutches of the Wicked Witch of the West and helps rescue Dorothy from the witch's castle. He is also the one to discover that the Wizard is not a wizard at all. What an amazing little dog!

DOGS IN THE SPOTLIGHT ▪ Dogs have been amazing us with their performances for many years—in movies, on the stage, on television, and (from much earlier times) in circuses, carnivals, and country fairs.

Although not all dogs are equally talented, almost any healthy, intelligent dog (of any breed or crossbreed) can act, do tricks, perform athletic feats, or pose for photos.

Dogs do not learn to do these things on their own, of course. Behind every dog performer is a trainer. Each trainer may use a different method of teaching, but all agree on one thing: When a dog and a trainer know and trust each other, performing is fun —for both of them.

In some acts, dogs are encouraged to do *on command* what they do naturally—run, jump, fetch objects, bark, paw, scratch, sneeze, stretch, or yawn.

Other acts require much more training. It can take months for a dog to master the ''games'' of opening doors, jumping through closed windows, or limping as if its leg is hurt.

MOVIE DOGS ▪ Toto, a cairn terrier whose real name was Terry, was such a good little actor that he almost ''stole the show'' from Judy Garland and the other actors in *The Wizard of Oz.* Trained and directed by Carl Spitz, Terry became a movie star—as have many other dogs. You see them today in new movies and in old ones that are shown over and over in movie theaters, on television, or on videotapes.

In early movies there was Pete the Pup, a homely black-and-white dog (part terrier) with a black ring around one eye. Pete played a funny street dog in the *Our Gang* comedies (later called *Little Rascals*). One of Pete's best-known acts was to look scared or guilty when he was in trouble. He would lie down, put his

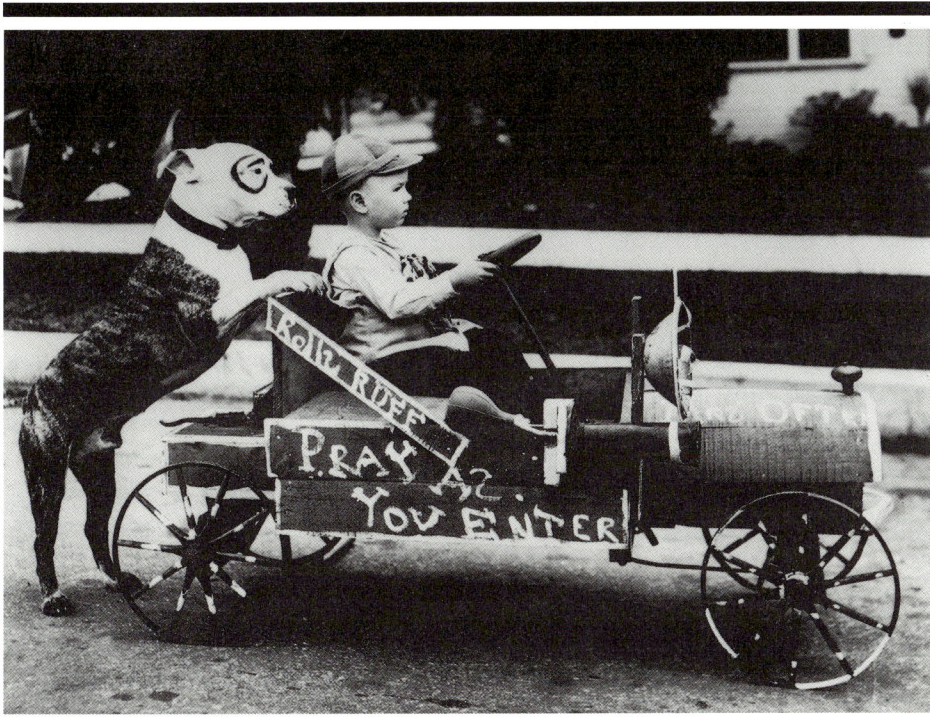

Pete the Pup performed many tricks in the *Our Gang* movies. Here he provides go-cart power for one of the "Little Rascals."

paws over his head, and close his eyes—as if he was saying to himself, ''Oh, no! Get me out of here!''

A German shepherd called Strongheart was the first great ''dramatic'' dog actor. His first movie, filmed in 1921, was *The Silent Call.* In one scene, Strongheart, who was (in the movie) half wolf, came back from a hunt to find his wolf family buried alive by an explosion. Stongheart looked so brokenhearted that audiences cried.

Rin Tin Tin, also a German shepherd, was the next dog to win the hearts of movie fans. From 1921 to 1931, "Rinty" was the first animal superstar of the movies. He was a strong, wise, lovable hero, always rescuing someone in the nick of time. Rinty's trainer, Lee Duncan, taught his dog more than five hundred commands.

Lassie became the next big canine (dog) movie star. Lassie should really have been called "lass-he," because the original Lassie (whose real name was Pal) and all the other collies who later played Lassie were male. Males were chosen because they were larger and had fuller coats than females.

In *Lassie Come Home* (the first Lassie movie), made in 1943, Pal showed what a good actor he was. In one scene, he dragged himself out of a river and fell to the ground. With his head between his front paws, he slowly closed his eyes as if worn out from swimming for miles. Actually, he had been in the water only a few minutes, following signals from his trainer, Rudd Weatherwax. When the scene was over, Pal jumped up, ready for a dog biscuit reward and whatever game Rudd wanted to play next.

Altogether, seven Lassie movies (six played by Pal) were made. Lassie was the first dog named to the American Humane Society's Hall of Fame.

Dogs have been just as popular in later movies as they were in the old Hollywood days.

Higgins (part cocker spaniel, part poodle, and part schnauzer) was a favorite of millions of moviegoers in the 1970s — and

In *Lassie Come Home,* Pal, as Lassie, was called upon to express all kinds of emotions. Here he and his co-star play a sad scene.

The trainer Frank Inn with Benji. The warm relationship between a dog and its trainer is the key to a great performance.

is still a favorite on video. In *Benji*, he played the part of a clever dog who saves his owners from kidnappers.

Higgins's facial expressions were almost human. In action, Higgins never took his eyes off his trainer, Frank Inn—one of Hollywood's top trainers. In the same way Rudd Weatherwax directed Pal, Frank would stand behind the camera, a dog biscuit in his pocket, and act out Higgins's part with him. When Frank acted happy, Higgins looked bright and alert. When Frank acted sad, Higgins's face drooped. When Frank looked angry, Higgins frowned. Other Benji movies followed, but Higgins played only in the first one.

In 1989 a big, bumbling French mastiff played the part of Beasley in a movie called *Turner and Hooch.* In one scene the dog had to jump through a window. Beasley was trained gradually—first to jump through paper (which tore easily), then through cellophane (a bit tougher), then plastic (tougher still), then glass that was invisibly cracked to break without hurting the dog.

Breakaway glass is just one of the many tricks moviemakers use to make things look different on the screen from what they really are. In a Stephen King horror movie called *Cujo,* the dog Cujo, a Saint Bernard, is supposed to be a vicious attack dog. In some scenes, to make him look especially gruesome, his coat was rubbed with dirt and his jaws were smeared with dripping gelatin, as if he were drooling.

Another Saint Bernard star, Beethoven, came to fame with a completely different image. In two family comedies, *Beethoven* and *Beethoven's 2nd,* this lovable dog appeared to almost destroy an entire household with his romping, drooling, and highly entertaining ''accidents.''

William R. Koehler trained animals for Walt Disney movies for twenty-one years. He taught a smart Old English sheepdog to

The sight of an Old English sheepdog driving a car in *The Shaggy Dog* always got a lot of laughs from movie audiences.

play the part of Chiffon in *The Shaggy Dog*. The sheepdog had to learn to ride in a wheelbarrow, climb out a high cellar window, ''drive a car,'' and do many other things a dog would not normally do.

STAGE DOGS ▪ On the stage is a New York City street scene. Annie, a little girl who has run away from an orphanage, meets a sad-looking stray dog with a ragged coat and floppy ears. The dog is running away from a dogcatcher.

''Come here, Sandy,'' Annie calls, making up the dog's name because of his color. She needs a friend.

Sandy goes to her, crawling timidly on his belly. He is afraid of strangers but he, too, needs a friend.

Just as the two are getting acquainted, a cop shows up.

''Run, Sandy, run!'' Annie yells. She can tell that Sandy is an orphan (like herself), and she does not want the dog to be taken to the dog pound any more than she wants to be captured.

Sandy scurries offstage. Annie, however, is caught and returned to the orphanage. Only at the end of the play—after Daddy Warbucks, a kindly rich man, rescues Annie from the orphanage—are Annie and Sandy together again.

Sandy, the star of the musical *Annie,* was trained by Bill Berloni, who really did rescue the lovable part-terrier dog from a dog pound. Bill taught Sandy all the moves needed for the play. To crawl, Bill got Sandy to lie down, then Bill lay (lightly) on the dog's back. Next, he took hold of Sandy's front legs and moved them back and forth, repeating the word ''Crawl!'' Sandy finally got the idea after dozens of tries.

Sandy played his part from 1977 to 1983 and became one of Broadway's biggest stars—with his own private dressing room and his own car to take him to and from the theater.

Sandy the Broadway celebrity poses with his *Annie* co-star Aileen Quinn.

The play *Annie* was so successful it was followed by another musical called *Annie Warbucks.* The sequel continued Annie's life, adopted by Daddy Warbucks. Another lovable shaggy dog was found for the part of Sandy. This time, it was a female named Cindy Lou.

Many other dogs have had stage careers. A huge Saint Bernard played Nana, a "nurse" to the Darling children in the play *Peter Pan.* A small dog (part spitz) played Rusty, a daredevil tightrope walker in the musical *The Will Rogers Follies.*

Many people are eager for their dogs to become stars. For the part of Asta in *Nick and Nora,* another musical, about 150 wirehaired terriers tried out. Asta not only had to look perky but also be able to bark whenever a phone rang, to "sing" on cue, and to carry things around in his mouth without dropping them. It took many days to find the perfect actor.

TELEVISION DOGS ▪ A big family dog named Dreyfuss lopes into the living room just as a guest in the house starts to sit down. The dog firmly nudges the guest away from the chair.

Dreyfuss's owner explains: "That's Dreyfuss's chair."

The guest quickly moves, and Dreyfuss lumbers into the chair and flops down, eyeing the guest triumphantly. The dog is clearly an important part of the family.

A dog named Bear (part Saint Bernard, part golden retriever) played the part of Dreyfuss in the television program *Empty Nest.* Bear was chosen because of his shaggy looks and because he could, on cue, act "disapproving" or "charming." In the series, Dreyfuss was sometimes called on to raise his eyebrows when people talked—as if saying, ''What a dumb thing to do!'' Bear was good at that, but he was not a very energetic dog. So his lively look-alike brother, Julio, was hired as a ''stunt dog'' to act for Bear in scenes where Dreyfuss had to run or jump.

A basset hound named Cleo played in an earlier series called *The People's Choice*. She was a ''talking'' dog (with a person off-screen saying the words). Frank Inn, Cleo's—as well as Benji's—trainer, taught her to fall over backward, walk on her hind legs, stand on her head in the corner, arch her back and bark like a seal, among many other surprising acts.

More and more dogs have become television actors since the fourth Rinty starred on television in *The Adventures of Rin Tin Tin* in the 1950s. That series ran for nineteen years, and Rin Tin Tin programs are still on the screen. Lassie starred in a television series that ran for seventeen years. In a later series, the role was played by the first Lassie's seventh grandson!

Today you see dogs on television in situation comedies (sitcoms), daytime dramas (soap operas), dramatic series, television movies, and in dozens of commercials.

DOGS IN ADVERTISING ▪ Because people who buy cars, clothes, furniture, and other products are often dog lovers, dogs can frequently sell things better than people can. Some dogs have become famous because of their work in commercials.

One of the earliest dogs to advertise a product was a fox terrier named Nipper. A picture of Nipper showed the dog sitting

Dreyfuss shares a quiet moment with the actor Richard Mulligan on the set of *Empty Nest.*

Nipper, who once appeared in advertisements for RCA Victrolas, has been joined by Chipper in television commercials.

and listening, with cocked head, to the sound of ''his master's voice'' coming from an RCA Victrola (an old-fashioned record player with a horn for a speaker). That one picture sold many Victrolas for the company.

A funny-looking bullterrier called Spuds MacKenzie (who in real life was a female named Evie) not only made television commercials but got to be so popular that his (her) picture was printed on T-shirts and coffee mugs and other such items.

Bashkim Dibra has trained many dogs for commercial work —as well as for movies and television programs. ''In advertising,'' Dibra says, ''dogs often work on platforms, posing for photographs or performing an act. For platform work, a dog has to stay quietly in place while you give it signals from as much as twenty feet away.''

Trainer Bashkim Dibra surrounded by some of his many star performers.

Since wide-awake expressions are favored for advertisements and commercials, ''Bash'' (as trainer Dibra is called) gets his dogs to look lively (head cocked, ears perked up, eyes sparkling) by smacking his lips, clapping his hands, or squeezing a squeaky toy.

CIRCUS DOGS ▪ Lights! Music! Clowns! Acrobats and Animals! Right now, all eyes are on the center ring where a small white dog is climbing a ladder—eighteen rungs high.

Step by step, up goes the little fox terrier. He wobbles and climbs on, wobbles and climbs. The higher he goes, the louder the music plays. The whole audience holds its breath. Will Tippi make it to the top?

A bright spotlight follows Tippi's every move. Then, just as he puts a paw on the platform, one of Tippi's rear legs slips off a rung.

The crowd gasps, ''Ooooohhh!''

Tippi hangs on and scrambles onto his high perch.

The crowd breathes again: ''Aaaaahhh.''

On the ground beneath the platform, two people hold open a small blanket.

Tippi hesitates, peering down, turns away as if the sight scares him. Then suddenly he leaps. He hurtles straight down, lands in the middle of the outspread blanket, and is lowered to the ground. The audience whistles and claps. Tippi leaps to his feet and, nearly wagging his tail off, turns this way and that, taking bow after bow. A real circus star!

Circus dogs excel at many tricks, from simple jumps
to daring high-wire acts.

It took a long time for Tippi to learn his climb-and-leap act. He started by spending weeks practicing on a stepladder. First he was taught to stand on his hind legs and put both front feet on the highest rung he could reach. Then, one by one, he pulled his hind legs onto the lowest rung. He repeated this all the way to the top. His trainer encouraged him by saying ''Up! Go up!'' and by holding treats over his head.

At first, the trainer had to lift Tippi's hind quarters to the next rung. But finally Tippi became an expert on the stepladder. He was then given higher ladders to climb — right up to eighteen rungs.

Many circus dogs are trained to be acrobats. Around the ring they go, riding on ponies' backs (on a special pad). They climb on top of barrels and roll them across the ground. They jump rope. They turn somersaults, frontward and backward. They walk tightropes.

Some dogs — often dressed up in hats, pants, or masks such as rabbit ears or elephant heads — do funny skits with clowns. They zigzag between clowns' legs each time a clown takes a step. In one daring act, a poodle is tossed from a seesaw to land on its front paws on a clown's hands, its hind legs high in the air.

Tippi was an actor as well as a performer. He was trained to pretend to wobble, to let his back foot slip on purpose from the top rung of the ladder, and to hesitate (as if scared) before jumping into the blanket. His "being in danger" made the act much more exciting than if he had just scooted up the ladder and jumped. (Had he really slipped, he would have been caught.)

Some circus dogs do "smart dog" acts.

"How much is two plus two?" asks the dog's partner.

The dog barks four times.

Wow! A dog that does arithmetic!

Actually, of course, the dog does not know how to add, subtract, multiply, or divide. It has learned to watch its trainer for a signal. At the right number of barks, the trainer might either lift an eyebrow, point a finger, nod, or smile. The dog immediately stops barking. A real genius!

Some "smart dogs" can "read."

"Where's the CAT?" asks the dog's partner.

The dog picks up a flash card with the word CAT on it.

"That's *right*," says the partner. "Is the cat awake or ASLEEP?"

The dog picks up the ASLEEP card.

A trainer "reads" to her pupils. Many tricks can be used to make it appear that dogs can recognize the written word.

"Very good," says the partner. "Now, do you want to have dinner or go out and PLAY?"

The dog picks up the PLAY card. The trick here is that each card is scented with a different odor—such as a cat food smell (for CAT), perhaps a hay smell (for ASLEEP), and a tennis ball smell (for PLAY). The dog was trained to sniff for the card that goes with the word. Some dogs learn dozens of words in this way.

PERFORMING-ANIMAL PROTECTION ▪ Dogs that perform in show business sometimes work hard (with frequent rests), often under hot spotlights or in noisy, confusing places. But the animals are not abused. Their trainers see to that. Performing animals are also protected by organizations such as the ASPCA (American Society for the Prevention of Cruelty to Animals) and the American Humane Association.

When the movie *Homeward Bound: The Incredible Journey* was made, for instance, members of the American Humane Association and the Oregon (where much of the movie was shot) Humane Society were careful to see that the filmmakers treated the animals kindly. And, of course, their trainer, Tammy Maples, would never have allowed any abuse!

In *Homeward Bound,* Sassy (a Himalayan cat), Chance (a black-and-white bulldog pup), and Shadow (a golden retriever) cover miles of mountainous country trying to find their way home. They cross a dangerous river, where Sassy falls in. They meet a porcupine that leaves sharp quills in Chance's nose. They

In *Homeward Bound,* two dogs and a cat complete a
treacherous journey over miles of dangerous terrain.
In reality, of course, it was all acting and movie magic.

also meet a skunk, a bear, and a mountain lion that chases them
over rocks. The three animal friends barely escape being hit by a
train, and Shadow injures his leg when he tumbles into a deep,
muddy pit.

How could that movie be made without the animals being in
danger? If you watch the movie very closely, you'll see that, in
most shots, when the three friends "meet an enemy" the camera

shows first the dogs or cat, then the "enemy." Actually, they are each filmed individually and are not near each other at all. When Sassy is "swept away" by the river, you'll notice that you see *something* (not really the cat) being hurtled downstream; all the quick shots of the wet cat are close up—perhaps taken in a pool of swirling water. You can be sure that Sassy was not in the water much longer than it would take to get a good bath.

Later, the film is cut and spliced (put together) to make it look as if each escape is a terrifying experience. Not so.

THE AWARDS ▪ Dog stars are honored for their work. The Patsy (Performing Animal Top Stars of the Year) awards have been given to animal stars every year since 1951. Like movie Oscars, stage Tonys, and television Emmys, Patsys honor actors (including dogs, cats, horses, chimpanzees, rabbits, and even a pigeon and one jaguar) for outstanding performances.

Movie-dog winners (named by their roles, not their real names) have included Wildfire in *A Dog's Life,* Spike in *Old Yeller,* Big Red in *Big Red,* and Duke in *The Ugly Dachshund.*

Both Rin Tin Tin and Lassie won Patsy awards for their work in television series. A dog called Scruffy won the Patsy for his work in the Chuck Wagon Dog Food commercial. Sandy won the 1978 award for his stage role in *Annie.*

THE REWARDS ▪ Many dog stars earn enormous salaries (which, of course, go to their owners, who are usually their trainers). Some Hollywood dogs live like movie stars, dressing up for par-

This dog's
a star, and
he knows it.

ties (usually for publicity) in gold-plated collars or fancy vests or ruffs. There is no limit to the toys and treats they can have: a full-sized plastic fire hydrant, for example, or six crates of tasty biscuits.

But, in fact, most famous dogs live quite ordinary lives. When they are not performing or being ''interviewed'' by the press, they stay quietly at home with their trainers. They are well loved, well fed, well cared for—and always ready for the next call: ''Ready, action, *go!*''

Easy Tricks to Teach Your Dog

SHAKING HANDS
from trainer Bashkim Dibra

Sit the dog facing you, on leash.

Say "Give me your paw" or "Shake hands."

Tap the dog's chest, gently but firmly pull its leash up, without jerking it. At the same time, pick up the dog's right paw in your right hand.

Repeat "Shake hands" until the dog responds.

Give the dog lots of praise when it gets the idea, and soon it will shake hands on its own.

JUMPING
from trainer Arthur J. Haggerty

With the dog on leash, jump over a board placed across a doorway.

Say "Over" as you get the dog to follow you.

Repeat until the dog can jump off leash.

Next level: Put a hoop in the doorway. With the dog on leash, draw the leash through the hoop.

From the far end of the room, say "Over. Come." Repeat until the dog will come through the hoop off leash.

Gradually raise the hoop as high as the dog can jump.

DANCING (for small dogs)
from trainer Bashkim Dibra

Sit the dog facing you, on leash.

Dangle a treat over the dog's head, and gently but firmly pull up on the leash, without jerking it.

Say "Up, dance" until the dog is able to stand steadily on its hind legs.

Move your leash hand in a circle, clockwise, saying "dance" to get the dog to turn while on its hind legs.

Give the dog lots of praise—plus a treat. Soon it will perform at the "dance" command.

FURTHER READING

Baer, Ted. *How to Teach Your Old Dog New Tricks.* New York: Barron's, 1991.

Berloni, William and Allison Thomas. *Sandy, The Autobiography of a Star.* New York: Simon and Schuster, 1978.

Dibra, Bashkim. *Dog Training by Bash.* New York: Penguin, 1992.

Foster, Joanna. *Dogs Working for People.* Washington, D.C.: National Geographic Society, 1972.

Haggerty, Arthur J. and Carol Lea Benjamin. *Dog Tricks.* New York: Doubleday, 1978.

Javna, John. *Animal Superstars.* Milwaukee, Wisc.: Hal Leonard Books, 1986.

Machotka, Hana. *The Magic Ring.* New York: Morrow, 1988.

Weatherwax, Rudd. *The Story of Lassie.* New York: Duell, Sloan and Pearce, 1950.

INDEX